6061

P9-BZI-135

North Portico, undated LIBRARY OF CONGRESS

North Front, Main Entrance, undated LIBRARY OF CONGRESS

THE
WHITE HOUSE

Leonard Everett Fisher

Holiday House/New York

South Portico and Wings, viewed from the Washington Monument, 1952 NATIONAL ARCHIVES

Quentin Roosevelt on Algonquin, 1902 LIBRARY OF CONGRESS

"I don't think that any family has ever enjoyed the White House more than we have," wrote Theodore Roosevelt, twenty-sixth president of the United States. He may have been right. The Roosevelt children, Theodore, Jr., Kermit, Archibald, Ethel, Quentin, their half-sister Alice, and a small army of friends—the "White House Gang"—not to mention their pet bear, snake, raccoons, dogs, cats, and a calico Shetland pony named "Algonquin"—cavorted everywhere in and out of the mansion. They chased each other endlessly around the attic or roller-skated up and down the slick corridor floors. Their whooping and hollering echoed through the building. Once Quentin squeezed Algonquin into the elevator and brought him to Archie, bedridden with the measles. Sometimes their father joined in the fun. Their mother, Edith, remained unruffled amid all the chaos. "A nervous person had no business around the White House . . . ," Chief Usher Erwin H. "Ike" Hoover later re-marked. He had spent forty-two years in the White House, serving in various capacities during the Harrison, Cleveland, McKinley, Roosevelt, Taft, Wilson, Harding, Coolidge, and Hoover administrations.

There were other presidential children who turned the White House into their own amusement park—Buck and Jesse Grant, Willie and Tad Lincoln, Irwin and Abram Garfield, Amy Carter, and more. The Garfield boys used the vast emptiness of the East Room to stage pillow fights while riding tricyclelike contraptions called "velocipedes."

Not every president or his family enjoyed being in the White House, however. William Howard Taft, former secre-tary of war, governor of the Philippine Islands, and "Teddy" Roosevelt's successor, thought that the White House was the "loneliest place in the world." He would rather have been

White House Police roll call with Archie (left) and Quentin (right) Roosevelt, 1902 LIBRARY OF CONGRESS

8

appointed to the Supreme Court than elected to the presidency.

Millard Fillmore, thirteenth president, called the White House a "temple of inconvenience."

About a hundred years later, Harry S. Truman, thirty-third president, viewed the mansion as a "great white prison." But Truman, his wife Bess and their daughter Margaret did not have to live in the White House during most of Truman's second term. They lived across the street in Blair House, on the other side of Pennsylvania Avenue, while the White House underwent extensive renovations. The mansion was then 150 years old, and badly in need of repairs.

When Calvin Coolidge, the thirtieth president, was told some twenty-five years before the Truman reconstruction that the White House roof was a dangerous thing to be under, he dryly pointed out that while he himself never wanted to live under it in the first place, there were plenty of other people willing to take the risk.

The first to complain about "this great castle" were its earliest residents, John Adams of Massachusetts, second president of the United States, and his wife, Abigail. Four months remained of Adams's one term when he moved into the unfinished, cold, and damp mansion on November 1, 1800. Depressed by the rawness and her rheumatism, Abigail Adams, who joined him two weeks later, complained that all she did was "shiver . . . surrounded by forests . . . that wood is not to be had because people cannot be found to cut and cart it." Yet, John Adams established the importance of the "President's House" and what it represented the day after he and Abigail arrived. Expressing his deepest feelings in a letter to Abigail, he wrote:

I Pray Heaven to Bestow
The Best of Blessings on
THIS HOUSE and on ALL that shall hereafter
Inhabit it. May none but Honest
And Wise Men ever rule under This Roof!"

In July 1790, a ten-mile-square swampy area was chosen to be the site of the capital of the United States of America. Until then, New York and Philadelphia were the temporary capitals of the young country. The land was located on the eastern bank of the Potomac River between Maryland and Virginia. It was in the newly created District of Columbia—named after Christopher Columbus. The area was not a state. It was a unique federal district set aside to carry on the business of government. It seemed that the northern states did not want a capital in the slaveholding southern states. Likewise, the southern states did not want a capital in any of the northern states. Most members of Congress wanted the seat of government in a quiet place far removed from crowds of complaining citizens. The Congress had already been threatened in Philadelphia by mobs of former Continental Army soldiers who demanded their unpaid wages.

The problem was solved by Secretary of the Treasury Alexander Hamilton and Secretary of State Thomas Jefferson. They encouraged Congress to agree to placing the nation's capital in a remote area far away from crowded cities, not too far north, not too far south, and acceptable to all members of Congress. President George Washington himself chose the ten-square-mile site for the District of Columbia and the new city which would bear his name—"Washington." He knew the region, since his home, Mount Vernon, was only eighteen miles downriver. Earlier he had helped plan the city of Alexandria, which would be bordered by the southern edge of the new city. In 1791, President Washington commissioned French aristocrat, engineer, and architect Major Pierre Charles L'Enfant to design the streets, parks, and buildings of the new capital. L'Enfant had served on Washington's staff during the Revolutionary War. Included in L'Enfant's assignment was the selection of a site and design for the president's "Palace," an official residence that most Americans preferred to call "House." They did not want to be reminded of the British royalty from which they had so recently won their independence.

L'Enfant convinced himself that President Washington needed an enormous, elaborate building fit for an emperor. In his certainty he would not allow anyone to interfere with his design. Even his patron, President Washington, found him difficult. What the president envisioned was a large,

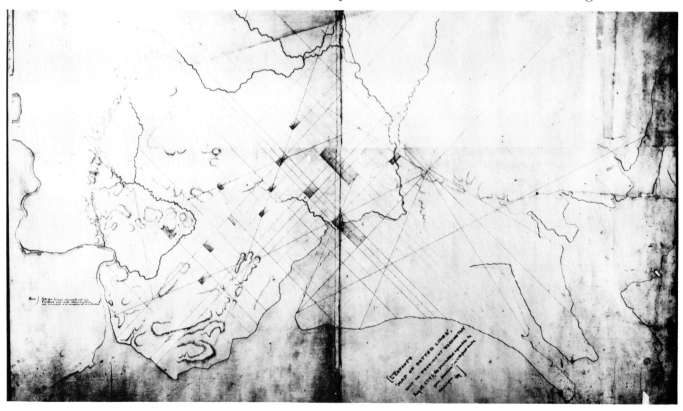

L'Enfant's plan of Washington, D.C., 1791 NATIONAL ARCHIVES

magnificent, richly appointed house, not a vast, ornate, royal palace. L'Enfant also ran afoul of Thomas Jefferson, who saw himself as an architect and one better able to design buildings for the federal city. There were others, too, who plainly disapproved of L'Enfant's extravagant designs. They seemed better suited to the tastes of French Queen Marie Antoinette who was about to lose her head over her own extravagances. L'Enfant was fired, but his plan for the city of Washington was kept. Jefferson's idea to fill it with great Roman-style classical buildings was dismissed, however, as being "too fancy."

Jefferson would not be put off. He convinced President Washington to hold a competition for the design of the President's House. He planned to enter it himself. On March 14, 1792, five hundred dollars or a gold medal was offered to "a person who before the fifteenth day of July next shall produce . . . the most approved plan . . . for a President's house to be erected in this city . . ." Nine plans were submitted. One of these was by Thomas Jefferson, who signed his entry "Abraham Laws." But L'Enfant's arrogance and Jefferson's meddling turned George Washington toward a young Irishman from South Carolina whom he had met on a trip through the South, architect-builder James Hoban. Hoban had impressed the president who encouraged him to come to Federal City—Washington—where he made his drawings virtually under the noses of the judges. The judges were the three commissioners who governed the District of Columbia. Anxious to please George Washington, they awarded Hoban the prize. Hoban chose to accept the gold medal instead of the five-hundred-dollar prize money.

The design as conceived by Hoban and modified by George Washington would create the largest and most luxurious home in America at the time. And it would remain so for

Jefferson's rejected design,
1792 LIBRARY OF CONGRESS

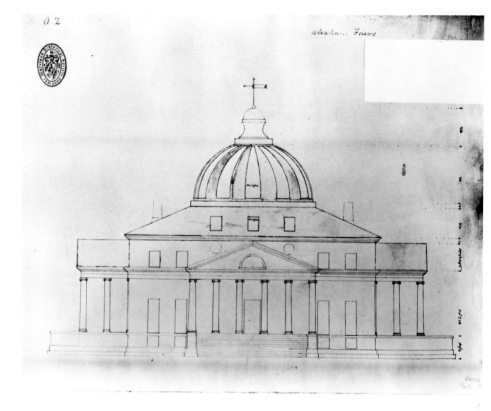

Hoban's winning design,
1792 LIBRARY OF CONGRESS

about seventy years. It was Washington's wish that the house be a proper residence and office of a president of the United States—"large-scale," he commented. He wanted the building and its grounds to be elegant and imposing. It mattered little to him or to anyone else in late eighteenth-century America that the house was somewhat unoriginal, adapted from other designs. Among the buildings that influenced it were Leinster House in Dublin, Ireland, and Château de Rastignac in southern France. In Washington's mind it was better to have part or all of the design modeled after some well-known, generally admired public building since public appreciation was proof of the building's permanence—and the country's permanence.

For the sake of the building's importance and permanence, it was necessary that it be made of brick faced with stone or just stone, rather than of wood or plain brick. From time to

Leinster House, Ireland LEONARD EVERETT FISHER

time Washington despaired that the house might not be big or magnificent enough for the future presidents of the country— a country that was sure to be larger than its current thirteen states and one district. As for his own future, Washington suspected that he might never live in the President's House. Elected America's first president in 1789, he would serve two terms and retire to Mount Vernon in 1797 where he died in 1799. The President's House would not be ready for occupants until 1800. Washington was destined to be the only president of the United States never to live in the mansion. Yet, the mansion owes its character and appearance more to George Washington than to any other person.

By March 1792, all land surveys had been completed for both the mansion and its extensive grounds—the President's Park. George Washington, having once been a surveyor himself, had assisted in the survey. Slaves, borrowed from nearby Virginia plantations, had already cleared the land. The southern view from the high ground chosen for the President's House was a long marshy and wooded vista thick with sycamore, oak, and cedar trees that sloped toward the Potomac River. Much of this acreage had been farms belonging to the Burns and Peerce families who sold them to the government. The wildlife in the area included deer, bear, pheasant, and other game birds.

Workmen staked out a rough building outline and landscaping scheme along a gentle ridge and began to dig into the red clay soil for the foundation. Meanwhile, stones for the foundation were hauled to the site from a quarry at nearby Aquia Creek. Scottish stonecutters imported from the British Isles went to work on them. The construction area quickly grew into a busy, rowdy shantytown where workmen lived, supplies were stacked, and tools were stored.

All during the summer of 1792, as Hoban worked over the design details, slaves labored to lay the foundation stones for the 170-by-85-foot mansion. By autumn the basement walls of the President's House began to appear. On Saturday, October 13, 1792, a procession that included city officials, craftsmen, laborers, and the general population marched from Fountain Inn in the village of Georgetown down dusty Pennsylvania Avenue to the southwest corner of the rising President's House. With speeches and ceremony, an engraved brass plate was set in mortar on a foundation stone. Over it was placed the cornerstone. It read:

> This first stone of the President's House was
> laid the 13th day of October 1792, and in
> the seventeenth year of the independence of
> the United States of America
>
> George Washington, President
> Thomas Johnson,
> Doctor Stewart,
> Daniel Carroll,
> Commissioners
>
> James Hoban, Architect
> Collen Williamson, Master Mason
>
> Vivat Republica*

After the ceremony, the marchers paraded back to Fountain Inn to celebrate in high style. The cornerstone brass plate has never been uncovered.

* Long live the republic.

James Hoban designed a three-floor, slate-roofed structure of thirty-six rooms. Seven of these rooms, together with a spacious entrance hall and cross hall or corridor, comprised the main or first floor—the "principal story"—a street-level floor entered at the North Front of the house facing Pennsylvania Avenue. The other twenty-nine rooms were divided between the second-floor family quarters—bedrooms, guest rooms, sitting rooms or parlors, a private dining room, and offices—and the basement or ground floor facing the south grounds on the South Front of the mansion. The ground floor contained the servants' waiting room, kitchen, and various service and storage rooms. Additional storage space was provided in the attic above the second floor. The several floors and attic were linked by three staircases which included an elegant grand staircase that connected the second-floor family quarters to the first-floor public rooms, and a dark,

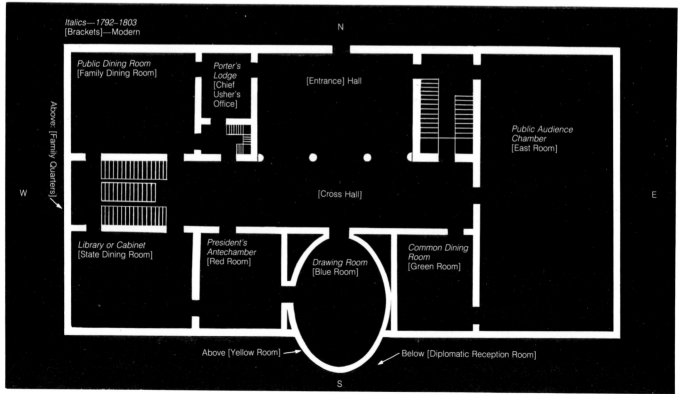

Floor plan, first floor, 1803 (after Hoban and Latrobe). The current room names are in parentheses. LEONARD EVERETT FISHER

narrow service staircase that twisted its way from the ground floor all the way to the attic.

The building's interior architectural grandeur was reserved for its stately public rooms on the main or first floor. Entering the President's House through the main entrance at the North Front, a visitor would pass a small room immediately to the right called the "Porter's Lodge." Here would be posted the doorkeeper, the caretaker who kept an eye on whoever came and went through the main entrance. For years doorkeepers ate, slept, and entertained their cronies in this room until 1869 when Julie Grant, the wife of President Grant, had it cleaned out and turned into an office for running the house—now the office of the chief usher. Just beyond the main entrance hall was the cross hall, a long colonnaded corridor that connected the great 82-by-44-foot ceremonial East Room to two rooms: the State Dining Room and what could have been a library but became instead a meeting room for the president's cabinet. In time the "Cabinet Room" would become the State Dining Room while the State Dining Room would become the family dining room. The Cabinet Room would be located elsewhere.

A graceful oval drawing room or "salon" to be used for receptions was planned for the South Front of the building directly opposite the main entrance hall. During the administration of Martin Van Buren, 1837–41, the room was decorated in blue and became known as the "Blue Room." The room was flanked on its east side by the common dining room which John Adams used as an overnight guest room and Thomas Jefferson made into his private dining room. James Madison used it as a quiet parlor while James Monroe had the room decorated in green, played cards there, and called it the "Green Room." John Quincy Adams left the room green but re-created it as a parlor in 1825. The room has been a parlor called the "Green Room" ever since.

On the west side of the oval Drawing Room and leading into the Cabinet Room was the Cabinet Waiting Room where members of the cabinet could relax before or after their meetings, or where official guests waited to be received by the president. The room, originally decorated in yellow, was first known as the "Yellow Drawing Room," or "Mrs. Madison's Parlor," during James Madison's presidency, 1809–17. Here, on Wednesday evenings, his wife Dolley threw Washington's most fashionable parties for the famous, near famous, and wealthiest people in America. The decorative cast of the room was changed from yellow to red during James Monroe's administration, 1817–25. From that time on the room was called the "Red Room" and used for light entertainment, musicales, and small parties.

The Blue Room is one of three oval rooms in the White House proper. Below it on the ground floor is the oval Diplomatic Reception Room which leads out to the south grounds from under the South Portico. Until the administration of President Martin Van Buren, this oval room was the servants' waiting room. Here, servants waited to be summoned by a series of bells attached to cords that ran through the house. The kitchen was across the hall, its smoke-blackened walls hidden by coats of whitewash. In 1840, President Van Buren had a central heating system installed in the White House which until then had been heated by fireplaces or wood stoves. The oval ground-floor waiting room became the furnace room. Now, no longer the furnace room, it is used to greet foreign dignitaries and other important guests who enter the White House through the South Portico entrance.

Diplomatic Reception Room, 1961 WHITE HOUSE HISTORICAL ASSOCIATION

On the second floor above the Blue Room is the oval Yellow Room where John and Abigail Adams held the first White House New Year's Day reception, January 1, 1801. It was not "yellow" then. In fact it was not even finished. Jefferson called the room the "Ladies' Drawing Room," or sometimes the "Ladies' Withdrawing Room." Dolley Madison had some yellow furnishings in the room which were lost in the 1814 fire. It wasn't until 1961–63 when Jacqueline Kennedy, President John Fitzgerald Kennedy's wife, redecorated the room in yellows that it was officially called the "Yellow Room." This particular oval room has been used over the years by presidential families as a parlor, for private receptions, and by presidents themselves to entertain heads of foreign governments before state dinners.

A fourth oval room, the present-day Oval Office of the president, is not in the White House. It was built in 1909 in the center of the Executive Office Building attached to the West Wing. It was later moved to the southeast corner of the Executive Office Building.

The building slowly developed in construction. Missing in the basic plan, however, were some practical necessities. There were no horse barns or servants' quarters, neither were there closets, bathrooms, or running water. As was the custom, outdoor wells provided water and outhouses served as bathrooms. The stables were two blocks east of the mansion. The servants slept where they could outside the White House grounds. The cooking was to be done, as was the custom of the day, in two open, smoky fireplaces forty feet apart and both framed by an assortment of pots, pans, kettles, and utensils. The house seemed to be the "temple of inconvenience," that was later described by President Millard Fillmore. Despite the lack of interior conveniences, the warm, tan

Oval Office, undated NATIONAL ARCHIVES

Virginia sandstone exterior was imposing.

When John Adams moved in during the afternoon of November 1, 1800, there were about 130 federal employees and 500 families in the District of Columbia. The President's House, although impressively large, was hardly magnificent. Rubbish was strewn everywhere. Builders' supplies and tools were stacked around the house. Sheds stood along the muddy grounds. The grand staircase had not yet been installed. And only six of the rooms were usable.

The ceremonial East Room was a cold, cavernous, drafty shell where Abigail Adams hung up her wet laundry to dry because there was "not the least fence, yard, or other convenience" outside. She also hung up the mansion's first work of art, a full-figure portrait of George Washington painted by Gilbert Stuart in 1797, in the first-floor Oval Room. During the next year, 1801, President Thomas Jefferson's secretary, Meriwether Lewis, curtained off the southeast corner of the East Room and used it as a bedroom-office. Lewis had to find space elsewhere when a leaky roof caused the ceiling to fall in. He finally left the mansion in 1804 to head an expedition with William Clark into the newly purchased Louisiana Territory. The East Room, meanwhile, remained unfinished for the next twenty-seven years.

Thomas Jefferson summoned Benjamin Henry Latrobe to design a new leakproof roof. He was the young architect of the Capitol Building, that, when finished, would be the immense structure where the laws of the new country would be made. Jefferson also appointed him surveyor of the public buildings of the United States. Latrobe was asked to design a roof that would not be as heavy as the slate roof that was now cracking the building's stone walls. Latrobe designed a lighter sheet-iron roof and replaced the slate. He stayed on to do

President George Washington by Gilbert Stuart, oil on canvas, 1797
NATIONAL PORTRAIT GALLERY, SMITHSONIAN INSTITUTION; ON LOAN FROM LORD ROSEBERY

other work, revising Hoban's earlier plan and trying to carry out many of President Jefferson's architectural projects for the mansion. Among these were high stone walls to encircle the grounds and shield the house from public view, an iron gate entrance and driveway approach to the North Front, another driveway approach to the South Front, East and West wings connected to office buildings on each side of the building, landscaping, and various room alterations.

Many of the projects never got further than Latrobe's drawing board. Others were begun and remained unfinished due to lack of money. What moneys there were for public building projects in Washington were being funneled into the completion of the huge Capitol Building. The stone walls of the President's House were begun but never finished, nor were the interior alterations. A North Front driveway, however, was completed. Both the East and West wings were built but never attached to office buildings. An icehouse, smokehouse, wine cellar, servants' quarters, stable, coach house, tack room, and outhouses were hidden from view in these wings. Jefferson had the exterior of the mansion whitewashed to prevent mildew and left the building to the next president, James Madison, and his wife, Dolley, in 1809.

For three years the Madison administration seemed to be better known for Dolley's stylish parties than for its hardworking president. Dolley took no political side when it came to entertaining. All, including the president's opponents, who loved a good time, good food, and wine and who represented the world of high fashion, the arts, literature, politics, or who were celebrated in some way were welcome in the happy Madison household. Dolley treated her guests lavishly.

But disaster struck the Madisons' fashionable presidency. In 1812, thirty-one years following the British surrender at

Yorktown which ended the War for Independence, Great Britain and the United States were once again at war. After American troops burned Canadian government houses in York (now Toronto), between 150 and 200 British sailors set fire to the President's House as well as to the Capitol Building.

The British had entered Washington during the early evening of August 24, 1814. A late summer thunderstorm threatened overhead. President Madison and some associates and servants had fled across the Potomac River into Virginia. Dolley Madison had left earlier, after first making sure that Gilbert Stuart's portrait of George Washington hanging in the East Room would be rescued. The now empty mansion was broken into by looters who took anything they could carry from silver urns to furniture. While much remained when the British entered the house, they took nothing from it except a souvenir or two of no value. Instead, they piled in the center of each room whatever they found and set fire to the house.

"Instantaneous conflagration took place and the whole building was wrapt in flames and smoke. The spectators stood in awful silence . . . ," remembered one eyewitness. As the fire burned, a thunderous storm fell over Washington and soaked the area with rain, but it was too late to save the President's House. It was a blackened, hollow ruin by morning.

The British left three days later. The president quickly returned to Washington where he was accused of being a coward and of humiliating the nation. At the end of January 1815, Andrew Jackson had beaten the British at New Orleans, England had lost the war, and all was forgiven. By March 1815, James Hoban began rebuilding the President's House.

Two years later, James Monroe, now president and living in the mansion, urged the restoration on to completion. The

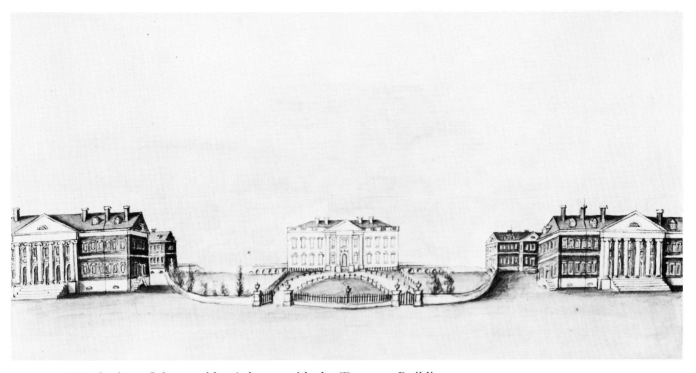

North view of the president's house with the Treasury Building
(left) and the War Department (right), 1821. Watercolor by
Baroness Hyde de Neauville. LIBRARY OF CONGRESS

work came to an end in 1820. Once again, the President's
House stood alive with stately grandeur. Still, the grounds
were barren and untidy, in need of work and landscaping. By
that time, the whitewashed building had provided the mansion with a popular nickname—"The White House." Not until
1902 and the onset of the twentieth century, during the
administration of President Theodore Roosevelt, would "The
White House" become its official name. Meanwhile, the
Monroes filled the house with French furnishings, food, and
wine, and left the East Room unfinished. They consulted
Bostonian Charles Bulfinch, the new architect of the Capitol
(which also had to be rebuilt after the fire) about the grounds.

In 1824, toward the end of Monroe's presidency, one of two
porticoes designed by Latrobe and Hoban four years earlier
was completed. Called the "South Portico," it was a circular
roof supported by columns. This seemed to have for its model

the portico of Château de Rastignac in France. The other portico on the North Front of the mansion—the North Portico—would be built five years later.

Little was done to the White House itself during the presidency of John Quincy Adams of Massachusetts, 1825–29, son of President and Mrs. John Adams. His four-year term was marked by the creation of ornamental gardens around the White House and the planting of trees and shrubs in Lafayette Square, a park facing the north facade of the White House. The presidency of John Quincy Adams marked the end of an era of luxury-minded aristocrats who maintained a standard of White House living that seemed unattainable to the swelling common population of the United States. Adams's aloofness kept him distant from the people who had little to say about presidential elections. They called him a "king" and a "monarch." He was soundly defeated by the hero of New Orleans, General Andrew Jackson, the people's choice, the first American president to have reached that high office after having been nominated by a national convention. And the people came to Washington from far and wide on Inauguration Day to celebrate the beginning of a new era in American politics.

Washington, thick with people, was awash in warm sunlight on that March afternoon in 1829. Tables of food, lemonade, ice cream, and punch laced with whiskey had been set out in the East Room. A frail Jackson, still mourning the recent death of his beloved wife Rachel, patiently received a steady line of distinguished visitors in the first-floor oval salon, a room then glowing with red decoration. Quickly the polite line of well-wishers turned into a crushing mob, not all of them distinguished.

"The Majesty of the People had disappeared," wrote Wash-

Chateau de Rastignac, France LEONARD EVERETT FISHER

ington matron Margaret Bayard Smith, ". . . a rabble, a mob . . . scrambling, fighting, romping. What a pity! What a pity!" Later, she wrote: "Ladies and gentlemen only had been expected . . . , not the people en masse. But it was the People's day, and the People's President and the People would rule . . ."

Good-natured mobs nearly blocked President Jackson's entry into the White House after his slow parade down Pennsylvania Avenue from the Capitol. The mob poured unchecked through the north entrance. Once inside the White House, it ranged through every corner of the mansion, damaging the furnishings. The president's aides had all they could do to protect the president and to keep the crushing sea of humanity away from him. The aides succeeded in dragging him through a window and safely away to a nearby hotel as the sound of breaking glass echoed around them.

When the Jackson staff took over the White House from John Quincy Adams, plans were immediately made to modernize the mansion. Not all of the plans were accomplished as quickly as Jackson first hoped. One of the proposed projects was to rid the house of dangerous candle-burning chandeliers and oil lamps. The latest type of lighting was gaslight. Gas was less likely to set a house on fire, but more likely to blow up a house from the ash of a misplaced cigar. The project never materialized during Jackson's presidency. An idea that did materialize, however, was the pumping of running water into the house. This had its advantages, from fighting fires to kitchen and personal use. White House baths, for example, had been uncomfortable affairs, typical of the times. Baths were taken either in the bedrooms or in a ground-floor bathing room with the bather seated in a tin or copper tub. Since there was no running water in the house, servants had been hauling buckets of well water to the bathers from the ground-floor kitchen where it was heated. Showers installed by Jackson were taken in almost the same way. Buckets of heated water were poured overhead into a contraption which released the water as a shower.

Three modernizing projects were put under way immediately: the complete furnishing and decorating of the East Room, the building of new stables, and the construction of the North Portico. Just as stone had been an essential element to George Washington in giving the President's house permanency and a look of importance, so was the Greek Revival North Portico essential to Andrew Jackson. In his mind it made the house a symbol of democratic power as derived from the ancient Greeks. Once again James Hoban supervised the work which was finished in 1830. Now the building, complete with its South and North Portico additions, and

North Portico before 1948

South Portico before 1948 NATIONAL ARCHIVES

gleaming with a fresh coat of white paint, appeared, for the most part, as we know it today. A year later James Hoban was dead. The pleasant architect-builder and protégé of George Washington died a wealthy man surrounded by his relatives and friends.

The only addition of real importance to the White House during New Yorker Martin Van Buren's single term, 1837–41, was the furnace. And to further keep the drafts from swirling around the main part of the house, a glass vestibule was added at the north doors. The glass enclosure had side doors so that no one would bring in the howling winds by entering the north doors directly. Other than that, President Van Buren, a widower, and his four sons, lived lavishly among their fashionable New York guests—and beyond their pocketbooks. Angelica Singleton Van Buren, wife of Abraham Van Buren, the president's secretary and eldest son, served as White House hostess. Angelica was the niece of Dolley Madison who lived across the street from the White House. Angelica sought her aunt's advice about White House entertainments.

The shortness of President Van Buren's four years in the White House could not be compared to that of his successor, President William Henry Harrison. The feeble sixty-eight-year-old Harrison, a general and former governor of the Indiana Territory, earned the nickname "Tippecanoe" in 1811 when he defeated the Shawnee Indians in the Battle of Tippecanoe Creek. Harrison was inaugurated on March 4, 1841, caught a cold, and died in the White House thirty days later, April 4, 1841. Harrison was the first American president to die in office. Never before had the White House been draped in black. The East Room was a scene of deep grief. There the president lay in state, his coffin resting on a table overflowing with black drapery.

John Tyler, Harrison's vice president, was now president. He moved into the White House with his partially paralyzed wife, Letitia, and some of their seven children in an atmosphere of disbelief. No one wanted to believe that a president had died in office. And no one wanted to believe that the vice president—especially an old-time anti-Jackson man—had rightfully become president. Protected by the Constitution, Tyler refused to be anything but the president. The challenges to his succession soon became threats. Tyler asked Congress for protection. On July 1, 1842, a White House Guard was established—four men—which would one day grow into the Washington Metropolitan Police Force. While in office, President Tyler made the White House the scene of glittering parties. He prevailed on the seventy-five-year-old Dolley Madison to manage these affairs. Mrs. Madison was only too happy to oblige. As for the White House: other than some new furnishings, turning the Green Room into a private sitting room, and maintaining a presidential office on the second floor, little changed during the Tyler years.

Over the next sixteen years, 1845–61, five presidents worked small changes in the White House that reflected the times, their taste or that of their wives and hostesses. War with Mexico raged, gold was discovered in California, and the Washington Monument was begun during the term of James Knox Polk, a small, unsmiling man from Tennessee who was served by his slaves from back home. His stature was so unassuming that his wife Sarah had the United States Marine Band play an old march "Hail to the Chief" at every formal occasion in order for him to make a presidential impression. Its playing has since become a tradition. He introduced gaslight and photography to the White House, and had a statue of Jefferson placed at the mansion's north entrance.

General Zachary Taylor, "Old Rough and Ready," hero of the Mexican War, served a year and died. He was the second president to lie in state in the East Room. During his term California became a state and Dolley Madison died, the last surviving connection to the Founding Fathers and the American Revolution. Vice President Millard Fillmore of New York filled out the remainder of President Taylor's term—not quite three years—and failed to be renominated. His wife Abigail, who believed that no home was complete without well-read books, founded the White House library. Also, during his term, the grounds were redesigned and White House security was tightened.

President Franklin Pierce, another Mexican War hero, came to the White House as issues of slavery and states' rights divided the country. There were fistfights in Congress and threats of assassination. President Pierce was never without a bodyguard. A glass greenhouse was built on the east side of the White House within sight of the unfinished State and Treasury Department building. It provided the mansion with fresh-cut flowers. Today, the White House flower "shop" provides fresh flowers. The plumbing and heating systems were updated. And never-before-seen objects brought back from Japan by Commodore Matthew C. Perry were exhibited in the Blue and East rooms.

President Pierce was followed in 1857 by President James Buchanan whose niece, Harriet Lane, ran a social calendar of glittering parties and balls. The greenhouse was taken down and a larger glass conservatory was built on the west side between the White House and the War and Navy Department building. Three celebrated events marked President Buchanan's term. John Brown, an antislavery fanatic, was captured after attacking the government arsenal at Harpers Ferry, Virginia. He was hanged on December 2, 1859. The following May 1860, a state reception was held in the East Room for the first Japanese officials to visit the United States. In September 1860, Albert, the nineteen-year-old Prince of Wales, the future King Edward VII of Great Britain, visited the White House. He was the first royal visitor to spend the night in the mansion.

Two months later, Abraham Lincoln was elected president. On April 12, 1861, Fort Sumter, South Carolina, was bombarded by forces of the Confederate States of America, a new Southern American government. The Civil War had begun.

Confederate troops of the "South" were just outside of Washington posing the threat of attack or invasion. Federal or Union troops of the United States government—the "North"—were camped everywhere in the city. Even the White House was an armed camp, with Union troops stationed on the grounds and in the East Room itself. Cannon fire could be heard across the Potomac River in Virginia as Union troops were being mauled at Manassas.

During the Lincoln administration, 1861–65, two funerals were held in the White House. On May 24, 1861, in Alexandria, Virginia, a Southern sympathizer shot twenty-four-year-old Colonel Elmer Ellsworth, a Lincoln law clerk, bodyguard, and friend of Lincoln's eldest son, Robert. Colonel Ellsworth's regiment had just secured the town for the safety of Washington. Ellsworth, who lived in the White House, received a state funeral in the East Room. On February 20, 1862, eleven-year-old Willie Lincoln lay in a coffin in the Green Room. He had died of a fever. People in Washington were constantly getting sick. Willie Lincoln's younger brother, eight-year-old Tad, was also sick with fevers as was

President Abraham Lincoln, 1860
by Hesler CHICAGO HISTORICAL SOCIETY

Earliest known photograph of the White House, 1860–61,
by Mathew Brady LIBRARY OF CONGRESS

John Nicolay, one of President Lincoln's two secretaries.

Cholera, malaria, and typhoid fever had plagued the swampy city for years. Not far from the White House a garbage-choked canal thick with flies and mosquitoes stretched from the Washington Monument to the Capitol Building. Its offensive odors drifted through White House windows, making the hot and humid Washington summers unbearable. John Hay, Lincoln's other secretary, called the White House the "White pest-house." From time to time Mary Todd Lincoln, the president's wife, went north to shop or to escape her critics. They accused her of extravagance and Southern loyalties since several members of her family were fighting with the South. While she was away, the president slept in the nearby Soldiers' Home and left the uncomfortable White House to his staff and servants. The smelly canal was filled in in 1872 and became a thoroughfare—Constitution Avenue.

Nothing of note was done to the White House during the melancholy war years. The conservatory was kept full of flowers and plants. The mansion—now officially called the "Executive Mansion"—was given a fresh coat of white paint. The paint smell combined with the odorous canal left everyone gagging for breath. The president insisted that all public buildings, the White House included, should look neat, trim, and as everlasting as the Union itself.

Upstairs, on the second floor, a hallway was created between the president's office and the oval room which had become the Lincolns' living room-library. Now the president could walk to his private quarters without being seen and waylaid by the crush of people waiting in an outer office. Beyond the oval living room-library were family and guest rooms. Among these on the northwest side was the Prince of

Wales Room where the British prince had slept on his recent visit. Thereafter, and until about 1900, the room became the State Bedroom for extraordinary visitors. It was furnished in a quietly grand manner. Its centerpiece was the eight-foot-long rosewood "Lincoln Bed." A century later, the bed and some of the room's furniture were moved to a guest room now called the "Lincoln Bedroom." Contrary to what many people think today, both the Lincoln Bedroom and the bed itself were never slept in by Lincoln. During Lincoln's administration, the bedroom was the Cabinet Meeting Room, where on January 1, 1863, just before the traditional New Year's Day reception, President Lincoln signed the Emancipation Proclamation putting an end to slavery.

The war ended on April 9, 1865. Confederate General Robert E. Lee surrendered to Union General Ulysses Simpson Grant. The North had won. Great celebrations were held

"Lincoln Bedroom," undated WHITE HOUSE HISTORICAL ASSOCIATION

throughout Washington. The White House was open to all visitors without special invitations. And the multitude came. Five days later, Abraham Lincoln was shot at Ford's Theatre by John Wilkes Booth, a noted actor. The president died the following morning, April 15, in a nearby boardinghouse. His body was returned to the Prince of Wales Room in the White House where a single bullet to his head was removed. The Lincoln White House years came to their sad end in the East Room where once again a president lay in state.

Now president, Andrew Johnson of Tennessee, Lincoln's vice president, conducted the nation's business in an efficient, humorless, no-nonsense way. However, he was a warm-hearted, tender soul in the company of his family—his ailing wife, Eliza, sons Robert and Andrew, daughters Mary and Martha, and five grandchildren, all of whom lived in the White House. President and Mrs. Johnson focused their private attentions on children and grandchildren—theirs and everyone else's—and spent much time allowing their daughter, Martha Johnson Patterson, to alter and renovate the mansion.

The entire place was cleaned, redecorated, reupholstered, recarpeted, whitewashed, repainted, and polished. The East Wing, which had begun to rot, was torn down. A new east entrance to the grounds was created. A fire destroyed the conservatory on the west side but a new conservatory was built. The second floor was rearranged to include a telegraph office next to the president's own office. Now, no one, least of all a president, had to take the long walk to the War Department to read the latest dispatches. The president's offices were in the southeast section of the White House where presidential offices had been located on the second floor since John Quincy Adams's time. The president even had a barber chair installed in the family quarters on the mansion's west side. The president was determined to have the White House stand as a postwar symbol of Reconstruction in the same way that Abraham Lincoln wanted to lift the nation's low wartime spirits with a fresh coat of paint.

Even though President Johnson was embroiled in bitter political battles, he made the White House an exciting scene of dinners, parties, and celebrations. In 1869, when he turned the White House over to his successor, General Ulysses S. Grant, the victorious commander of the Union armies, the White House was in the best shape it had been since the days of Andrew Jackson.

Under President Grant and his wife Julia, the staff was increased to create a more leisurely workday for the president. Grant preferred to make public appearances, ride his horses, chat with his old military pals, and play billiards to putting in a hard day at the office. Some of his staff lived in the White House in the comfort of the family quarters, while others lived in ground-floor dormitories. The furniture was once again restyled and rearranged. The parties went on, too—but always after the youngest children, Nellie, Jesse, and Buck, had been sent off early to bed.

The renovations continued and seemed endless. The grand staircase was replaced by a relocated grander staircase. The White House lobby was redone with patriotic themes, colors, and decorations. The statue of Jefferson on the North Front was removed to the Capitol and replaced by a flower bed. The Grants surrounded themselves with millionaires and generals either in the State Dining Room, the Red Room, or the Billiard Room. Included were the president's father-in-law, Judge Frederick Dent, a Southerner who tormented the president's father, Northerner Jesse Grant, and various guests, with insulting remarks about the North. The elder Grant refused to live in the White House, but Judge Dent had a room to himself there. Cigar smoke hung like a perpetual fog. No one talked politics. The Grants wanted the White House to be an untroubled place, free of the pain of the Civil War and the stormy political battles of Andrew Johnson. Their greatest social triumph was the marriage of Nellie Grant to a wealthy Englishman, Algernon Sartoris, May 21, 1874, in the newly decorated East Room. Its creaky seventy-four-year-old floor was propped up underneath by thick wood beams. A sumptuous banquet awaited the family and a few guests in the State Dining Room.

President Grant was asked to run for an unheard-of third term, probably by those who were profiting from the president's friendship. Grant refused. He had had enough. His administrations had been plagued with scandal, although he himself was a well-meaning and honest head of state, and he was ready to step down. The election that followed in 1876 was between Democrat Samuel J. Tilden of New York and Republican Rutherford B. Hayes of Ohio. It marked the one hundredth birthday of the United States. It was an election steeped in controversy. Tilden received more votes but an Electoral Commission declared Hayes the winner. Fearing that the Democrats would try to take over the government by force, President Grant, who was himself a Republican, arranged to have Hayes secretly sworn into office. The simple ceremony was held in the Red Room while a farewell dinner in honor of President Grant and his wife was in progress in the State Dining Room.

President Hayes made few changes in the White House. He was content to leave things as they were. He and his wife Lucy Webb Hayes, now called the "First Lady of the Land," or just

White House servants, 1877 RUTHERFORD B. HAYES PRESIDENTIAL CENTER

plain "First Lady," filled the White House with presidential portraits. Beginning with Mrs. Hayes, wives of American presidents would be called "First Lady."

A telephone and typewriter were added to the president's second-floor office. The typewriter was put to use immediately. The telephone was practically useless. Few people in the country had telephones. There was hardly anyone to call. For the most part, the Hayes presidency was smooth and pleasant. A minor flap occurred when the First Lady refused to allow alcoholic drinks in the White House—only soft drinks, like lemonade. Everyone called her "Lemonade Lucy."

Hayes was succeeded in 1881 by his close friend, James A. Garfield. But Garfield's presidency lasted only six months. He was shot and mortally wounded in Washington's Union Station. During the first four months, there were the usual receptions and public appearances. Some redecoration was begun. During the two months the president lay dying, a system for cooling the mansion was tried, chiefly to ease his suffering, but nothing changed in the White House. There was little time. Once again the White House was draped in black. This time, however, the president's remains lay in state in the Rotunda of the Capitol at the request of the First Lady, Lucretia Garfield.

Widower and Vice President Chester Alan Arthur took the oath of office as the twenty-first president at 123 Lexington Avenue, his New York City home, in September 1881. By December, he was in the White House with his two children, Nell and Alan, and feeling uncomfortable.

He did not want to be president, and he did not like the White House's interior decoration. As much as he wanted to change it, he had to suffer the completion of Lucretia Garfield's rearrangements because the work was already under contract when President Garfield died. To make matters worse, the White House was falling apart. President Arthur wanted to tear it down and erect a new building. Congress passed a bill to demolish the historic mansion, but no one had the heart to do it. The eighty-one-year-old President's House would stand and President Arthur would live in it—but not without major repairs, redecoration, and reconstruction.

The most interesting decorative pieces that were added to the mansion during the Arthur administration were New York artist-craftsman Louis Comfort Tiffany's colored glass screens in the main entrance hall. Tiffany's colored glass objects were the height of fashion during the 1880s. He went on to decorate most of the public rooms in the White House.

President Arthur was succeeded by Grover Cleveland, the only president to serve two terms that were not consecutive, 1885–89 and 1893–97. Benjamin Harrison, President William Henry Harrison's grandson, came in between, 1889–93.

The White House had a happy burst of life when President

Tiffany screens, 1883 LIBRARY OF CONGRESS

President Benjamin Harrison's office with *Resolute*
desk, 1889 (see page 86) LIBRARY OF CONGRESS

Conservatory, 1889 LIBRARY OF CONGRESS

President Harrison's son Russell with Harrison grandchildren, 1890. Left to right: Mary Harrison McKee, Russell, Benjamin Harrison "Baby" McKee, Marthena Harrison with pet goat "His Whiskers" and unidentified dog LIBRARY OF CONGRESS

Grover Cleveland, a bachelor, married Frances "Frank" Folsom in the flower-filled Blue Room on June 2, 1886. Music for the occasion, as for most White House occasions during the past thirty-five or forty years, was provided by the red-jacketed Marine Band. On this wedding day the band was led by John Philip Sousa, the "March King."

Except for repairs, fresh paint, fresh wallpaper, and a good cleaning from attic to basement, the White House remained largely unchanged during President Harrison's stay. Caroline Scott Harrison, the First Lady, worked hard to spruce up the mansion which had grown dingy during President Cleveland's first term. The furniture was rearranged, as were the uses of the second-floor nonpublic rooms. New pieces of furniture were purchased, worn pieces were sold. The First Lady had hoped to enlarge the White House by making it into a four-sided building with a parklike center. The plan failed to be approved by Congress. Perhaps the most noteworthy additions were electric lighting and a flagpole on the roof. President Harrison's administration came to an end with the death of his wife and the reelection of Grover Cleveland.

President Cleveland and his young wife returned to the White House on March 4, 1893, the parents of an infant daughter, Ruth. Another daughter, Esther, was born in the White House the following September. She was the only child of a president born in the mansion. The Clevelands left in 1897 after rearranging the furniture and painting various rooms—once again—to suit their own taste. They did not like the White House and fled at every opportunity. They spent much of their time in nearby suburban homes they owned or in their summer retreat at Buzzards Bay on Cape Cod, Massachusetts.

The White House reached its one hundredth year during

Red Room, 1893–1902 with portraits by Daniel Huntington of Mrs. Benjamin Harrison, President Rutherford B. Hayes, and relocated portrait of Mrs. Hayes

Green Room, 1893 with portrait of Mrs. Rutherford B. Hayes
by Daniel Huntington LIBRARY OF CONGRESS

East Room, 1893 LIBRARY OF CONGRESS

the administration of President William McKinley, 1897–1901, the Ohio governor who succeeded Grover Cleveland to the presidency. President McKinley was as ill-fated as any president could be. His wife Ida never quite recovered from the loss of two young children, a war broke out with Spain a year into his presidency, and he was assassinated. McKinley coped with the war from the Cabinet Room located between his office and the oval room on the second floor. The Cabinet Room eventually became the president's office. A presidential desk carved out of the timbers of the British man-of-war *Resolute* remained in the second-floor oval room. It was given as a farewell gift to President Hayes by Great Britain, and he left it in the White House. In the end, President McKinley was shot on September 6, 1901, by an assassin, Leon Czolgosz, as he stood in a reception line in Buffalo, New York. He died eight days later. The White House had entered its second century.

The only room in the White House to receive a complete overhauling during McKinley's administration was the Blue Room, the scene of so many presidential events and receptions. More lighting was added around the room and to the chandelier at the room's center. The wall panels and furniture shimmered in various shades of new blue silk. Moldings and other panelings were painted an ivory tone. The overall style of the room was eighteenth-century Colonial-American.

The late President McKinley's vice president, Colonel Theodore Roosevelt, the Spanish-American War hero, breezed into the White House with his family, their pets, servants, and maids to begin seven and one-half hectic years. The White House was so cramped for space that parts of the attic were used to house the maids. There were not even enough bathrooms for everyone.

Blue Room, 1899

State Dining Room, 1900 LIBRARY OF CONGRESS

The nation was growing fast and was ready to take its place as a world leader. The energetic Roosevelt symbolized America on the move. He had the "Lincoln Bed" moved to his bedroom. Dinner talk in the family's private dining room always turned to American history. The president kept up a steady chatter about the history of the White House. He enjoyed living in the mansion, and he enjoyed being the president. From the very beginning of the Roosevelt years, the White House was full of people coming and going. And Roosevelt made it plain that the White House belonged to every American when he sent a dinner invitation to Booker T. Washington. Washington, a former slave, now a prominent educator, was the first black person to dine at the table of an American president. Roosevelt was bitterly criticized for the invitation.

Also, during the Roosevelt years, plans were drawn up for the redesigning of Washington. Some politicians suggested that a new mansion be built and put somewhere else. "The President should live nowhere else but in the White House," said Theodore Roosevelt. The plans for a new building came to nothing. Instead, President Roosevelt set in motion other plans for improving the White House. With ample money from the Congress and designs by architect Charles F. McKim, a major White House renovation was completed in December 1902. The approach from the east, the East Front, was reconstructed, making it the main entry to the White House for social events. The glass conservatory on the west side gave way to an Executive Office Building connected to the main house by the West Wing colonnade. Offices were established there for the president, his cabinet, staff, and newspaper reporters. Roosevelt, however, continued to use the old second-floor office near the oval Yellow Room. A tennis court

East Front Gate House, undated LIBRARY OF CONGRESS

East Front, 1909 LIBRARY OF CONGRESS

was built on the south side of the Executive Office Building. The game had first come to the United States from Great Britain in the 1870s. Both the West and East wings were remodeled to look alike.

Parts of the crumbling inside were torn out, strengthened, rebuilt, and redecorated, including the grand staircase. Tiffany's glass screens were removed and later sold. The State Dining Room was enlarged to accommodate President Roosevelt's many dinner guests. The Red, Blue, Green, and East rooms were repaired, replastered, repapered, and redecorated. Four years later, on February 17, 1906, the East Room would be the scene of daughter Alice's wedding to Congressman Nicholas Longworth before a thousand guests. The old kitchen on the ground floor became a furnace room. A new kitchen was built. Some of the furniture was restyled. Other pieces were replaced as were drapes, moldings, and fixtures.

White House Office Building and Tennis Court, 1909 LIBRARY OF CONGRESS

Kitchen, 1909 LIBRARY OF CONGRESS

Nothing was left untouched. Even the second-floor family quarters were completely redone and refurnished. But despite all the renovations, the mansion in 1902 appeared as it always had been—and always would—the stately, elegant, and historic residence of the president of the United States.

William Howard Taft became president in 1909. By the end of his term in 1913 he would ride in an automobile instead of a horse-drawn carriage, an airplane would fly over the White House, America would have an income tax, and a new office for the chief executive—the "Oval Office"—would open its doors in the middle of an enlarged and redesigned Executive Office Building. The Oval Office would become the center stage in America of national and world affairs for the next eighty years, serving as the president's office through at least fourteen administrations.

During these four years, President Taft and the First Lady, Helen Herron Taft, celebrated their twenty-fifth wedding anniversary with the grandest White House lawn party ever given. At least eight thousand guests attended on the evening of June 19, 1911. Thousands more watched from afar. The entire White House and its grounds were lit with colored electric lights and lanterns from one end to the other, top to bottom—every flagpole, tree, shrub, and structure. The bulbs were strung so closely together that night became day.

The mansion's cheerfulness lingered as the Wilsons moved in in 1913—President Woodrow Wilson, Ellen Louise Axson Wilson, the new First Lady, and their daughters, Jessie, Eleanor, and Margaret. On March 15, a few days after the inauguration, the president began the White House tradition of regularly scheduled presidential news conferences. The Wilsons, as expected, quickly remodeled the family quarters and made plans for third-floor bedrooms and baths in the

Wright Brothers' "Flying Machine" over the South Lawn, 1911 LIBRARY OF CONGRESS

attic. Both Jessie and Eleanor—Nell—were married in the mansion, Jessie to Francis Bowes Sayre in the East Room, Nell to her father's treasury secretary, William Gibbs McAdoo, in the Blue Room. Shortly thereafter, Ellen Wilson died, World War I broke out in Europe, and gloom descended on the White House. But life came back to the mansion when the president married Edith Bolling Galt, a Washington, D.C. widow, sixteen months later. Preoccupied by international crises and America's entry into the war in Europe, President Wilson divided his time between the new Oval Office and his second-floor study. The study, once the Cabinet Room that served ten presidents either as an office, extra office, or study, is now the Treaty Room.

Mrs. Wilson, meanwhile, established the Presidential Collection Room in 1917 next to the Diplomatic Reception Room on the ground floor. The room was intended to display the countless gifts that poured into the White House. Now called the China Room, it was redecorated in 1970 by Mrs. Nixon.

Life in the White House during World War I was quiet and businesslike. Security was strict. People could not come and go as they pleased. Everyone had to be checked by the Secret Service or the Metropolitan Police. Clock winders, for example, who had come and gone on a regular basis without appointments since the days of James Monroe, were no longer admitted. The job of winding the White House clocks was done by military personnel or the reduced White House staff. So many of the staff had joined the war effort that there was no one left to cut the wide lawns. Instead, sheep were used to nibble at the grass and keep the lawns trim.

The war, national and international politics took their toll on the president. He spent his final days in the White House as an invalid, having suffered a stroke.

Sheep grazing on the South Lawn, 1919 LIBRARY OF CONGRESS

The Warren Gamaliel Harding White House years, 1921–23, were marked by the president's own standard of economy. He and the First Lady, Florence Kling Harding, brought their own furniture from Marion, Ohio, to the family quarters. Otherwise they left the White House as they had found it. However, they continued the traditional receptions and dinners. Among the traditions the Hardings relished was the annual children's Easter Egg Rolling event on the South Lawn begun in 1879 by President Hayes. It was always a wonderful party attended by thousands of Washington, D.C., children on Easter Monday. America was in a good mood. The president was content to make speeches, play poker with his friends, and leave the running of the country to the Congress. He died in San Francisco on August 2, 1923, while on a cross-country speaking tour.

New Englander Vice President Calvin Coolidge took his

Easter Egg Roll on the South Lawn, 1921 LIBRARY OF CONGRESS

oath in Vermont and filled out the remainder of the late President Harding's term. But once again tragedy stalked the White House. The president's youngest son, sixteen-year-old Calvin, Jr., died of blood poisoning from an infected blister in July 1924, just before his father's victory in the November election. The Coolidges—First Lady Grace Goodhue Coolidge, son John, and the president—bore their grief in stony silence. By spring 1925, the First Lady was ready to return to a livelier social life in the White House and made known her plans to redecorate the entire mansion in a Colonial style. The president, reacting to public criticism of Mrs. Coolidge's plans, disapproved and only allowed money to be spent on the redecoration of the family quarters. Besides, there were more pressing problems. The White House roof was in such bad shape it was ready to cave in. Worse still was the attic floor which was not originally designed to hold both the weight of the additional rooms put there during the Wilson years and the numerous items stored there. The attic floor was ready to fall in on the family quarters below. The Coolidges had to move out in March 1927 to a temporary home in Washington. By September, the ceiling of the family quarters, attic, and roof had all been rebuilt with steel. New rooms were created in the attic, now the third floor. And a glass-front Sun Room or "Sky Parlor" was built on the roof of the South Portico. Before leaving the White House to President and Mrs. Herbert Hoover in 1929, Mrs. Coolidge had the Green Room, designed by Charles F. McKim twenty-five years earlier, redone in her favorite Colonial style.

President Herbert Clark Hoover served one term, 1929–33. Like their predecessors, the president and First Lady, Lou Henry Hoover, moved furniture around, remodeled, and assigned rooms to suit themselves. But the Hoover years were haunted by the Great Depression when banks failed and millions of people lost their jobs and homes. The trouble was signaled by the stock market crash on October 29, 1929—"Black Tuesday." It was further accented by a fire that destroyed the Executive Office Building, including the Oval Office, on Christmas Eve, 1929, as the president looked on. By April 1930, the Executive Office Building and West Wing were rebuilt.

As the Great Depression began to devastate the American economy, the Hoovers tried to assure a discouraged America that everything would turn out all right. They held the traditional New Year's Day receptions and state dinners. The public was urged to take the regular mansion tours. Mr. Hoover was the first president to try and calm a nervous America with frequent speeches over the radio, but he could not withstand the tide of resentment toward his administration. He was as much voted out of office in 1932 as Franklin Delano Roosevelt was voted in.

The crisis that gripped the nation so preoccupied President Roosevelt and his aides, some of whom were permanent guests in the White House, that no one paid much attention to any social calendar during FDR's first one hundred days of what would become a twelve-year presidency, 1933–45.

The White House family quarters were constantly crowded with the president's family, friends, and aides—First Lady Eleanor Roosevelt, four sons, a daughter, daughter-in-law, grandchildren, the children of his friends and aides, various relatives, and on occasion his mother, Sara Delano Roosevelt. All of the Roosevelts were related to former President Theodore Roosevelt. Franklin Roosevelt, a polio victim who had to wear steel braces around his shriveled legs and be confined to a wheelchair most of the time, made the White House the

Executive Office Building fire, 1929 LIBRARY OF CONGRESS

focal point of his activities. Hardly a week had passed following his inauguration when he began a series of "fireside chats"—radio talks—to buoy the hopes of the downcast American people. Many of these broadcasts were made from the ground-floor Diplomatic Reception Room which did not then have a working fireplace.

While the president's time was immediately taken up with measures to rescue the financially immobilized nation, Eleanor Roosevelt moved in truckloads of the family's furniture from their home in Hyde Park, New York. She was bent on making the White House as comfortable as possible. And in the pattern set over so many years, upstairs studies became bedrooms and bedrooms became studies. Also, she saw to it that the president would have a steady stream of visitors from every walk of life, since his paralyzed legs would prevent him from getting out and walking or mingling with people all over the country. The ever-crowded White House gave the president a sense of what the American people thought. The president did leave the White House on frequent train trips, but it remained for the First Lady to travel the country as the president's eyes, ears, and legs.

The most meaningful change to come over the White House was the addition of a swimming pool in June 1933. Located in the colonnade connecting the White House to the West Wing, it was reached from the main house and the Rose Garden. The pool was built at the president's request and financed by public subscription, mostly by the people of New York. The pool was a health measure to keep Roosevelt fit with the only exercise he enjoyed—swimming. A movie theater was added to the East Wing.

Another change was the redesigning, tearing down, and reconstruction of the Executive Office Building. The work of

Christmas at the White House, undated
Seated left to right: Eleanor Roosevelt; Sara Delano Roosevelt, the president's mother; Mrs. Franklin D. Roosevelt, Jr. holding Franklin III; President Roosevelt; Mrs. John Boettiger, the president's daughter, holding her son John; Mrs. J. R. Roosevelt, the

president's sister-in-law; Mrs. John Roosevelt. Standing left to right: Franklin Roosevelt, Jr.; John Roosevelt; John Boettiger. Seated on the floor: granddaughter Eleanor "Sistie" Dall; Diana Hopkins, daughter of commerce secretary Harry Hopkins; and grandson Curtis "Bussie" Dall, Jr.

The Oval Office of President Ronald Reagan, 1981–89

the executive branch of government had become so complex that the president's staff had become larger than ever. The Executive Office Building, rebuilt in 1930 after the Christmas Eve fire, was no longer adequate. A new Executive Office Building was constructed during the latter part of 1934 where the previous one had stood. Its appearance from the outside was no different from the earlier structure, in keeping with White House architectural ideals rooted in the past. The interior, however, was renovated to have many more conveniences. The Oval Office was moved from the center of the building to a position where it opened out onto the Rose Garden. Work continued on other parts of the now 130-year-old-plus White House. A new kitchen was built as was a new library. Various other public or state rooms were given some attention.

The work was moving along until the afternoon of December 7, 1941, the day that will "live in infamy," when Japan attacked United States forces at Pearl Harbor in the Hawaiian Islands. America was suddenly and without warning drawn into World War II, which had been raging for two years in Europe. The White House became the nation's command post with high-ranking military officers and civilian officials coming and going day and night. A temporary bomb shelter under the Treasury Building and connected to the East Wing by a tunnel was hastily constructed. Later, a permanent bomb shelter was built under the East Wing.

Visitors from abroad came to confer with the president, including the British Prime Minister Winston Churchill who seems to have tried out nearly every bedroom in the mansion. For the next three years the American conduct of the most destructive war in history was decided in the White House, chiefly in the top-secret basement Map Room. Here the

North Front, December 7, 1941 LIBRARY OF CONGRESS

president received and sent messages to his commanders wherever they were on the world's battlefields. And here the president could follow the course of the war's events almost as soon as they took place.

The president had already been elected to an extraordinary third term in 1940. In 1944, FDR was elected to an even more unheard-of fourth term. Five weeks after his fourth inauguration Allied armies were within a month of delivering a crushing defeat to Germany, but Franklin Roosevelt was denied the final victory. He was dead at his favorite retreat in Warm Springs, Georgia. Franklin Roosevelt had been president and had lived in the White House longer than any other president.

Vice President Harry S. Truman became president and moved into a creaky White House with the new First Lady, Bess Truman, and their daughter Margaret in April 1945.

President Harry S. Truman buys a Veteran of Foreign Wars "Buddy Poppy" from Margaret Ann Forde, daughter of a wounded World War II Veteran, 1945 LIBRARY OF CONGRESS

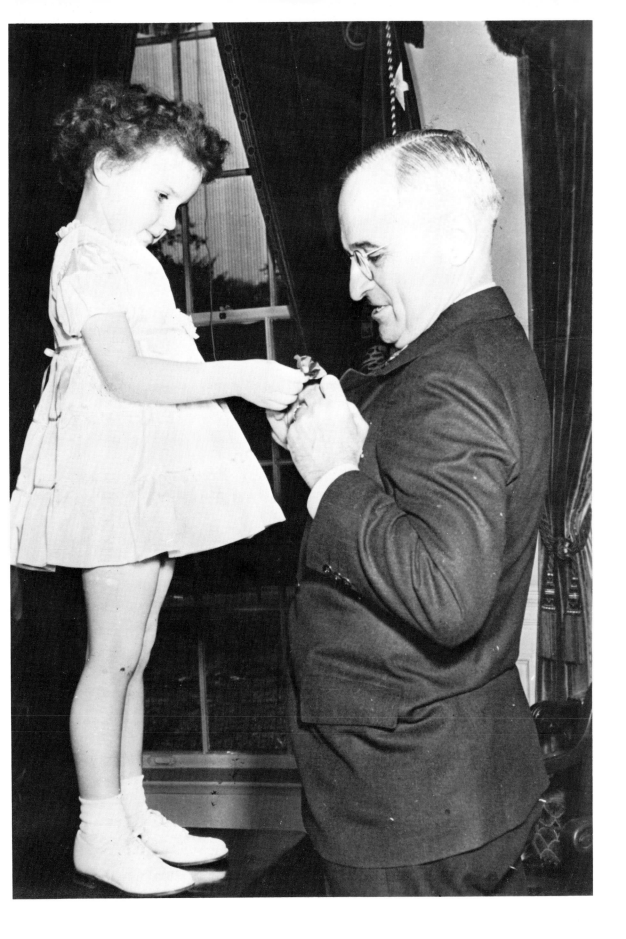

The unprecedented activities and constant flow of people that surrounded FDR before and during the war years left the White House worn and tattered. The Trumans spruced up the family quarters with a coat of paint, new wallpaper, and furniture. Also, the president had a number of projects in mind that he thought would make the White House more comfortable as well as more interesting. One of these was the addition of a second-floor balcony to the South Portico in 1948. It was a porch that could be reached from the oval Yellow Room and the family bedrooms. Called the "Truman Balcony," the president was severely criticized by those who believed he had defaced the original architecture.

However, by 1948, it was evident that the renovations, additions, and repairs made over the years had weakened the mansion's structural engineering and made the building an unsafe place in which to live. The mansion sagged. Some cracked walls were beyond repair. Everything from electric wiring to plumbing was wearing out. The mansion was 148 years old. Its original supporting timbers had to be replaced. The steel beams from the 1902 renovation were no longer reliable. Parts of the house vibrated when too many people were collected in a given area. The walls were beginning to shift because the mansion had become top-heavy and unsafe. Margaret Truman's parlor floor had nearly collapsed into the family dining room on the first floor. A study revealed that the White House was "falling down." The Trumans moved out.

After some nine months of planning, the White House was completely gutted. Not a floor was kept. Only its original stone walls were left standing. Much of the historic interior was removed and crated for future reassembly. Four years later President Truman and his family moved back into a brand-

Gutted White House interior after 1948 WHITE HOUSE HISTORICAL ASSOCIATION

new White House. Its structure had been reengineered to make the mansion safe, sound, and fireproof with more living conveniences and comfort for its residents. Its interior had been somewhat altered again. There were two new bomb-proof subbasement floors sunk deep into a new foundation. For the most part, these floors contained service rooms and shops necessary for the upkeep of the mansion. The grand staircase was redesigned to give the president a more spectacular entrance when descending from the family quarters to the first floor on state occasions. The family quarters had more closets, bathrooms, and guest areas than before. What had once been thirty-six rooms and then forty-eight was now fifty-four. The great public and ceremonial rooms—the East Room, State Dining Room, Blue, Red, and Green rooms appeared not to have changed at all. The Diplomatic Reception Room on the ground floor now had a working fireplace. And no longer did the mansion sag, crack, and creak.

President Truman left a sparkling new White House in January 1953 that seemed not to have suffered through the stresses and strains of a century and a half of hard use. Consequently, very little architectural alteration took place over the next thirty-six years—through the Eisenhower, Kennedy, Johnson, Nixon, Ford, Carter, and Reagan administrations. The most noticeable changes took place from time to time in the decoration of various public rooms. The treatment of the rooms was more historical than in past years with authentic period furniture, art objects, paintings, and bric-a-brac.

Beginning with Mamie Eisenhower, President Dwight David Eisenhower's wife, the White House began to function as a museum as well as a residence and place of business.

From 1953–61, Mrs. Eisenhower restored the Diplomatic Reception Room in an early nineteenth-century manner. Her work in the Diplomatic Reception Room was continued by Jacqueline Kennedy, President John Fitzgerald Kennedy's First Lady, who added authentic scenic wallpaper. Mrs. Kennedy was a founder of the White House Historical Association established in 1961 to help the public better understand the historical significance of America's most famous house. She replaced much of what were copied period pieces with authentic pieces. She furnished such rooms as the new Treaty Room, for thirty-six years the second-floor Cabinet Room, 1866–1902, with largely genuine pieces from the Grant administration. Both Presidents John F. Kennedy and Richard Milhous Nixon used the room to sign important treaties. Other than these occasions the room today serves as a private meeting place. Jacqueline Kennedy showed off the

Jacqueline Kennedy prepares to tape a television program in the State Dining Room, 1962 WIDE WORLD PHOTOS

Treaty Room after 1961 WHITE HOUSE HISTORICAL ASSOCIATION

historic White House to the nation in a memorable television program, February 14, 1962.

During the Kennedy years, 1961–63, the White House not only became a museum by preserving the nation's past with original furnishings, paintings, and other works of art, it also became a performing arts center. The world's greatest dancers, musicians, singers, actors, actresses, poets, and playwrights appeared in gala East Room concerts and readings. But again the nation was shocked when on November 22, 1963, President Kennedy was murdered in Texas and the East Room, so recently given over to the joys of music, was returned to its sorrowful past as the dead president was brought home to lie there in state.

Lyndon Baines Johnson, President Kennedy's vice president, assumed the presidency. And for the next six years, 1963–69, President Johnson carried forward Jacqueline

President John F. Kennedy thanks cellist Pablo Casals for East Room concert, 1961 NATIONAL ARCHIVES

President Kennedy and son John, Jr. in the Oval Office
(note *Resolute* desk — see page 49), 1963 WIDE WORLD PHOTOS

Kennedy's plans for the interior furnishing of the White-House. In 1965, Claudia "Lady Bird" Johnson, the First Lady, dedicated the Jacqueline Kennedy Garden in her honor on the South Front of the East Wing. The president himself established a Children's Garden on the southwestern rim of the President's Park.

During the five years of President Richard M. Nixon's presidency, 1969–74, First Lady Patricia "Pat" Nixon supervised the redecorating of the major rooms on the first and ground floors and encouraged the collection of antique furniture and portraits of presidents and their wives. In 1971, Pat Nixon refurbished the ground-floor Vermeil or Gold Room adjacent to the China Room. Here, Mrs. Eisenhower had assembled the White House collection of antique silver and gold-plated service pieces.

The two administrations that followed—those of President

Patricia Ryan "Pat" Nixon
by Henrietta Wyeth Hurd,
oil on canvas, 1978
WHITE HOUSE HISTORICAL ASSOCIATION

Gerald Rudolph Ford, 1974–77 and President James Earl "Jimmy" Carter, 1977–81—did little to alter the physical or decorative appearance of the White House. Nevertheless, these two presidents and their First Ladies, Betty Ford and Rosalynn Carter, did much to bring historic American paintings and sculpture to the mansion. Perhaps the most interesting, if not the most significant piece, to come to the White House during the Carter years is the only known portrait—a wax miniature—of James Hoban, the mansion's original architect and builder.

The Reagan years, 1981–89, were mostly spent completing the decorations for the family quarters on the second floor as well as the third-floor attic. Not much attention had been paid to these areas after the Truman renovation was finished in 1952. The major part of refurbishing the White House for nearly thirty years had been aimed at the more public rooms and service areas. President Ronald Reagan and First Lady Nancy Reagan, whose favorite basic color scheme always included red, gave to the family quarters an elegant informality rather than a sense of history.

Starting in 1980 and continuing through the Reagan years, the White House was chemically stripped of thirty-two layers of paint, revealing the original golden-toned Virginia sandstone that had been put in place almost 190 years before. Also revealed were smoke stains from the fire of 1814. The warm glow of the unpainted mansion, together with the charred evidence of history, will once again be covered over with a gleaming coat of white paint.

As in almost every previous administration since John and Abigail Adams, the arrival of George and Barbara Bush on January 20, 1989, was heralded by the redecoration and refurnishing of the family quarters.

James Hoban (from the miniature) LEONARD EVERETT FISHER

President Ronald Reagan and First Lady Nancy Reagan
off to Camp David retreat, 1987 WIDE WORLD PHOTOS

The White House stands, however much altered and changeable, as the steady focal point of American political and cultural continuity. The mansion is America's first public building and its most familiar building, a government building owned by the people—all of the people. It is the only residence and office of a head of state anywhere in the world opened to the public free of charge, even on a limited basis. The White House has served as a symbol of American well-being, durability, family life, and democracy. It continues to serve as a reminder to the rest of the world of America's peaceful transference of power from one president to the next—power derived from the people as expressed in the life within a single home and workplace—the White House.

South Front Flower Garden and Pool before 1948

THE PRESIDENTS

1.	George Washington	*April 30, 1789–March 3, 1797*
2.	John Adams	*March 4, 1797–March 3, 1801*
3.	Thomas Jefferson	*March 4, 1801–March 3, 1809*
4.	James Madison	*March 4, 1809–March 3, 1817*
5.	James Monroe	*March 4, 1817–March 3, 1825*
6.	John Quincy Adams	*March 4, 1825–March 3, 1829*
7.	Andrew Jackson	*March 4, 1829–March 3, 1837*
8.	Martin Van Buren	*March 4, 1837–March 3, 1841*
9.	William Henry Harrison	*March 4, 1841–April 4, 1841*
10.	John Tyler	*April 6, 1841–March 3, 1845*
11.	James K. Polk	*March 4, 1845–March 3, 1849*
12.	Zachary Taylor	*March 5, 1849–July 9, 1850*
13.	Millard Fillmore	*July 10, 1850–March 3, 1853*
14.	Franklin Pierce	*March 4, 1853–March 3, 1857*
15.	James Buchanan	*March 4, 1857–March 3, 1861*
16.	Abraham Lincoln	*March 4, 1861–April 15, 1865*
17.	Andrew Johnson	*April 15, 1865–March 3, 1869*
18.	Ulysses S. Grant	*March 4, 1869–March 3, 1877*
19.	Rutherford B. Hayes	*March 3, 1877–March 3, 1881*
20.	James A. Garfield	*March 4, 1881–September 19, 1881*
21.	Chester A. Arthur	*September 20, 1881–March 3, 1885*
22.	Grover Cleveland	*March 4, 1885–March 3, 1889*
23.	Benjamin Harrison	*March 4, 1889–March 3, 1893*
24.	Grover Cleveland	*March 4, 1893–March 3, 1897*
25.	William McKinley	*March 4, 1897–September 14, 1901*
26.	Theodore Roosevelt	*September 14, 1901–March 3, 1909*
27.	William H. Taft	*March 4, 1909–March 3, 1913*
28.	Woodrow Wilson	*March 4, 1913–March 3, 1921*
29.	Warren G. Harding	*March 4, 1921–August 2, 1923*
30.	Calvin Coolidge	*August 3, 1923–March 3, 1929*
31.	Herbert Hoover	*March 4, 1929–March 3, 1933*
32.	Franklin D. Roosevelt	*March 4, 1933–April 12, 1945*
33.	Harry S. Truman	*April 12, 1945–January 20, 1953*
34.	Dwight D. Eisenhower	*January 20, 1953–January 20, 1961*
35.	John F. Kennedy	*January 20, 1961–November 22, 1963*
36.	Lyndon B. Johnson	*November 22, 1963–January 20, 1969*
37.	Richard M. Nixon	*January 20, 1969–August 9, 1974*
38.	Gerald R. Ford	*August 9, 1974–January 20, 1977*
39.	Jimmy Carter	*January 20, 1977–January 20, 1981*
40.	Ronald Reagan	*January 20, 1981–January 20, 1989*
41.	George H.W. Bush	*January 20, 1989–*

INDEX

(Italicized numbers indicate pages with photos.)

Northwest Front, undated LIBRARY OF CONGRESS

ACKNOWLEDGMENTS

I would like to thank Mr. Rex Scouten, curator and former chief usher of the White House, for vetting the manuscript in the interest of accuracy and for his invaluable assistance, guidance, and advice in researching so warm and complex a history as that of the White House. His personal touch, anecdotes, and encouragement made our quiet visit to the mansion thrilling, enlightening, and memorable. I would also like to extend my appreciation to Mr. Bernard J. Meyers, executive vice president of the White House Historical Association, for his assistance; to Mr. Leroy Bellamy of the Prints and Photography Division of the Library of Congress for his patience and help; to Mr. Fred Pernell of the National Archives Photographic Services for his special attention; and to his small army who carted box after box of historic photographs to me to examine; to my editor at Holiday House, Margery Cuyler, who kept me in focus as we searched the White House past in Washington and made possible what seemed to me at times to be impossible; and to my patient wife, Margery Meskin Fisher, whose life with me began in a president's house at 123 Lexington Avenue, New York.

In addition, I should like to thank the White House Historical Association, the Library of Congress, the National Archives, The National Portrait Gallery, the Rutherford B. Hayes Presidential Center, the Associated Press/Wide World Photos, and the Chicago Historical Society for permission to use the photographs appearing in this book.

Library of Congress Cataloging-in-Publication Data
Fisher, Leonard Everett.
The White House / by Leonard Everett Fisher; illustrated with photos and drawings
by the author. —— 1st ed. p. cm.
Includes index.
Summary: A history of the White House and its inhabitants from 1790, when a site
for the new capital was chosen, to the present day.
ISBN 0-8234-0774-8
1. White House (Washington, D.C.)—Juvenile literature.
2. Presidents—United States—History—Juvenile literature.
3. Washington (D.C.)—Buildings, structures, etc.—Juvenile literature.
4. Presidents—History. [1. White House (Washington, D.C.) 2. Washington
(D.C.)—
Buildings, structures, etc.]
I. Title.
F204.W5F54 1989
975.3—dc19   89–1990   CIP   AC
ISBN 0-8234-0774-8